MW01097897

This book is lovingly d
the brightest light

life:

My wife Michelle,
My dad Howie,
and of course,

DERBY!

8 Weeks

12 Weeks

7 Months

Follow Derby on Instagram: @derbypup

Derby Goes Home!

Written by Terri Squire

Illustrated by Jasmine "Jaszy" Smith

Copyright © 2021 Terri Squire

All rights reserved. No part of this book may be reproduced in any form without the prior written permission of the author, except in the case of brief quotations embodied in critical reviews and certain other noncommercial uses permitted by copyright law.

For permission requests, please contact the author at www.terrisquire.com

Written and Designed by Terri Squire
Illustrated by Jasmine "Jaszy" Smith
Polaroid background image by Alexandra Koch via Pixabay

ISBN (Paperback): 978-7368425-1-5
ISBN (e-book): 978-7368425-0-8

Printed in the United States of America
First printing edition 2021

www.terrisquire.com

On one special
autumn morning
near the end of fall,
a little golden pup was born.
The smallest of them all.

The barnyard animals
oinked and neighed,
the hens were all a-twitter;
for in the hay 9 puppies lay,
a wriggling puppy litter!

The little pup
grew fast and strong
and learned to play with others.
Soon the pup was bigger
than his sisters and his brothers!

Two people
came to say "Hello,"
and sat right down to play.
The puppy
thought they were so kind
and wanted them to stay.

The mama dog
came over then
and licked the puppy's head.
"I know you're happy here, my dear,
but go with them instead."

The puppy knew
the time had come
to finally leave the farm.
They lifted up the frisky pup
and held him in their arms.